Our new baby arrived today.
I'm a big brother now, hooray!

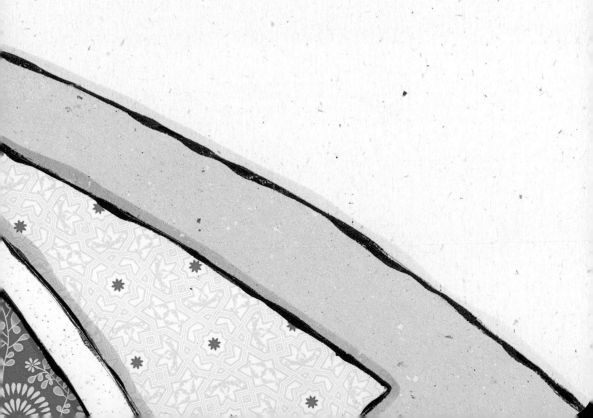

I used to be
a little baby, too.
But now I'm big!
Look what I can do!

I can help when baby feeds.
And always find what baby needs.

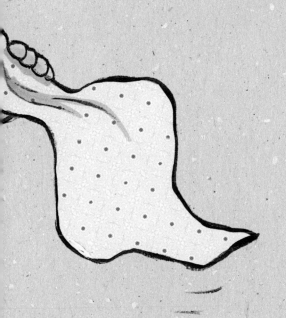

Dirty diaper, yuck! Let's see . . .

Here's a clean one found by me!

Mommy and Daddy say I'm clever
and that I'm the best big brother ever!

When we cuddle, the baby wriggles!
Give a tickle—baby giggles!

Splish-splash bath
is lots of fun!
Bubbles, washing,
and then we're done!

When baby sleeps, shhh, no noise.
I quietly play with all my toys.

But if baby wakes with cranky cries,
I softly sing sweet lullabies.

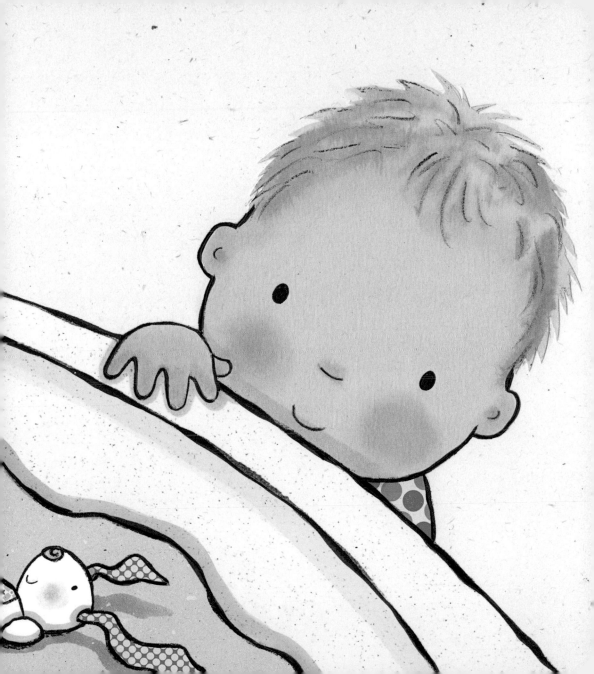

And as baby grows, we'll play together.
Because I'm a big brother forever!